THE ESCAPE

THE MARTIN RANCH SERIES: BOOK 3

AN OLD WEST NOVEL

WEST TEXAS, 1868.

BY: KENT HAMIILTON

Printed in USA

© Copyright 2020

All Rights Reserved

No part of this publication may be reproduced or transmitted in any form whatsoever, electronic, or mechanical, including photocopying, recording, or by any informational storage or retrieval system without express written, dated and signed permission from the author.

By reading this you accept these terms and conditions.

Table of Contents

Chapter One: "Run!" 5
Chapter Two: "Can you help?" 10
Chapter Three: "Meet the Family" 15
Chapter Four: "Happy to Help" 20
Chapter Five "Come With Me" 24
Chapter Six: "Hiding" 29
Chapter Seven: "Unexpected Kisses" 34
Chapter Eight: "A Proposal" 39
Chapter Nine: "We Need a Plan" 44
Chapter Ten: "Let's Go!" 49
Chapter Eleven: "This is Over!" 54
Chapter Twelve 59

Chapter One: "Run!"

Chloe struggled to keep her racing heart calm, worrying that John was going to wake up at any moment. This hadn't been the life she'd hoped for, and John wasn't anything like he'd said.

Creeping across the floor, Chloe paused with every squeak of the floorboards, but John's snores never stopped. He'd kept her here for three weeks now, with no mention of the pastor, and the way he was looking at her make her skin crawl. If she stayed, she was sure that he would force his way into her bed, and given how much bigger he was than her, Chloe did not think she would manage to fight back.

Her only plan had been to pretend as though everything was fine, and hope that one day soon, he might take her into town. Then, she could find the sheriff and demand that he help her. She hadn't seen another way out.

Then, John had begun to drink. It hadn't been too much at first but, as the days passed, he would drink more and more and Chloe's hopes had risen.

Finally, John had drunk himself into a stupor. He was now merrily snoring away, and Chloe had taken her chance. Thankful that she'd kept her one suitcase mostly packed, she'd hurriedly thrown everything else in and made for the door.

There key! It wasn't in the lock! Cursing under her breath, Chloe gently placed her bag down beside the front door and began to look around. It was already quite dark and, as usual, John had only lit one lantern, leaving the rest of the small farmhouse to be lit by the fire burning in the grate. Unfortunately for Chloe, the fire had already begun to bank and the flames were nowhere near as pronounced as they had been when John had first started drinking.

Where would he have put the key? Gritting her teeth in frustration and battling her fear, Chloe began to move quietly around the house, looking everywhere for it. It wasn't in the kitchen or in his bedroom, and he certainly wouldn't have put it in hers. The only other place was....on him.

Fearfully, Chloe walked towards John, taking in his sleeping features. His greying hair was in a complete mess, and the stubble on his chin was obvious. The man took very little care of himself, and expected Chloe to wait on him hand and foot – even without them officially marrying! It had all been like one horrible dream that Chloe hadn't been able to wake up from.

Looking over him, Chloe suddenly caught sight of his shirt pocket, which looked to have something inside it. Was it the key? Had he put it there so that she wouldn't be able to escape, even if he fell asleep? A shiver raced through her as she slowly reached out a hand and ran a finger lightly over the shirt pocket.

Yes, it felt like the key was there. Would he wake if she reached for it? *I'm not going to give up now.* Walking behind him, Chloe slowly reached one hand down over his shoulder, her fingers sliding carefully into his shirt pocket. The cool metal sent a jerk of hope through her, but the worst was not yet over. As she slowly lifted the key from his pocket, John stirred and stopped snoring.

"What's going on?" he mumbled, shifting in his chair.

Pulling the key out of his pocket, Chloe clenched it in one fist, before trying to speak calmly. "Nothing," she crooned, gently. "I was just coming to check you were all right." Pocketing the key, she carefully rested her hand on his shoulder, hoping the physical contact – which she had been so unwilling to give – would soothe him.

John grunted, and tugged her arm until she had no choice but to stand in front of him.

"Chloe," he slurred, pulling her bodily onto his lap. "You'll not get free without a kiss."

His breath stank and Chloe had to force herself not to turn away in disgust. Now that she had the key, she needed him to go back to sleep so that she could make her escape – and that meant doing anything she had to.

"Mmmm," she murmured, leaning forward and pressing a light kiss to his lips.

John growled with satisfaction and pulled her tighter against him, as his wet lips sought to find hers again.

Chloe tried not to tense, letting him kiss her just as he pleased. Eventually, his grip loosened and he pulled his head back, releasing her from his kiss. Wishing she could wipe her mouth with the back of her hand, Chloe tried to smile. "Go back to sleep," she crooned. "I'll be here when you wake up."

John mumbled something, reaching for the bottle of whisky on the table beside him. Taking a few long swigs, his eyes finally began to close once more, his hands loosening their grip on her body even more.

Taking slow breaths, Chloe waited for what felt like an eternity, before John began to snore again. His hands slipped down from her waist and thigh, leaving her free to carefully wiggle away from him. As quietly as she could, Chloe got to her feet, leaving John in yet another drunken sleep.

She felt dirty all over, wishing she could pour a bucket of steaming water over her head to clean her of his scent. His kisses had brought her nothing but revulsion, but her escape was just at hand. Walking quietly to the door, Chloe pulled out the key from her pocket and placed it in the lock. The squeak it made seemed to echo around the room, and Chloe held her breath as John shifted again in his chair. After a few agonising seconds, Chloe pulled open the door, keeping her eyes firmly on the sleeping John, before grabbing her suitcase and slipping out of the door.

The key still in her hand, Chloe bravely locked the door from the outside, throwing the key away into the darkness. If John woke up and discovered her missing, it might be the only thing that allowed her to make her escape.

Looking around, her heart still beating painfully in her chest, Chloe wondered what she was meant to do now. She hadn't thought this far ahead. Leaving the farmhouse was one thing, but there wasn't exactly anywhere else to go. She didn't know the area, or which direction the town was – but she did know she had to leave. Not able to risk taking a horse, she hefted her suitcase under her arm and stepped out into the night, picking up the small lantern she'd taken from the house. Hopefully, she'd find her way somehow, or at least be far enough away from John come the morning.

Chapter Two: "Can you help?"

Michael rubbed his eyes with the back of his hand, stumbling out into the cool air of the morning. The sun had only just begun to rise, but he was keen to make his way to the ranch.

"Got a horse?" he called, as the blacksmith glanced up from his work.

"You're up early," the man replied, grinning. "Going somewhere important?"

Michael shook his head. "Just heading out to the Martin Ranch. Been a long time since I've seen my brother."

"The Martin Ranch, huh?" the blacksmith replied, thoughtfully. "Seems they're just getting themselves back on their feet after what happened."

"What happened?" Michael asked, immediately. Christopher hadn't written to him with any news about the ranch for a long time, so whatever had happened must have been fairly recent.

The blacksmith shook his head. "Some of the old ranch hands decided to make trouble. They were thrown out for not listening to Miss Eliza, or Mrs Eliza as she is now. Tried to set the ranch on fire!"

Blinking a few times, Michael gaped at the blacksmith. "What? When? Is everyone okay?"

The blacksmith chuckled, slapping a hand on his shoulder. "Don't you start worrying now, everything's fine. One of the new ranch hands has a pretty plucky woman on his arm, and she raised the alarm. Managed to get the fire under control before it got too bad. Caught the men too! So everything's back to normal, but the ranch has taken a little while to recover."

"All the more reason to get out there," Michael muttered, grimly. When he'd written to Christopher, asking if perhaps he might have work for him, Christopher hadn't mentioned any difficulties at the ranch. The last thing he'd heard from him was that he'd gone and married the ranch owner, but hadn't claimed ownership of it from her. That sounded like his big brother, always doing the right thing. That was probably the reason he hadn't told him about the fire at the ranch, hadn't wanted him to worry.

"Here," the blacksmith said, leading out one of his horses. "Just bring her back in a couple of days, will you? Don't like my animals gone for too long."

"Thank you." Swinging up into the saddle, Michael dropped a couple of coins into the blacksmith's hand. "I'll make sure to have her back soon."

Michael enjoyed the feel of the wind on his face, feeling as though it were clearing the cobwebs from his mind. He'd been travelling for what felt like weeks, and now, finally, he was going to make it to his new home.

Life in the city wasn't what he'd hoped it would be. He'd spent his younger years learning the ways of the ranch and had thought he'd pursue a life of ranching the same as his older brother, but the call of the city had been too great. Unfortunately, it hadn't been as wonderful as he'd hoped and he'd ended up practically penniless, looking for a place to stay.

Thank goodness Christopher was able to help me out, Michael thought to himself as he rode across the plain.

A sudden shriek forced his horse to rear up, forcing Michael to cling on for dear life. Trying to hold on as best as he could, Michael calmed the horse and managed to keep his seat, all before realising what – or who – it was that had caused his horse to spook.

"What on earth do you think you're doing?" he exclaimed angrily, jumping down from his mount and glaring at the dust covered woman in front of him. "I could have been killed!"

"You should have watched where you were going," she retorted, although the slight tremble of her lip indicated just how exhausted she was. "I was simply sitting down for a moment."

He glowered at her for a moment more,

before admitting that she was right. He'd been too caught up in thinking about Christopher and Elizabeth to watch where he was going. "Are you going somewhere?" he asked, changing the subject. The woman in front of him looked utterly exhausted, as though she'd been out all night.

Chloe swallowed hard, not sure what she should say. She didn't know this man, and he could very easily be a friend of John's.

"I'm going to the Martin ranch if you need some help," Michael said, a little more gently. "It's not far."

Glancing up at him, Chloe took in the man's kind green eyes and honest face. He didn't look dangerous, and, at this point, she had no idea of where else to go. She'd stumbled around in the darkness for most of the night, before eventually falling asleep with her head on her valise, sheltered by a cluster of trees. Now that dawn was approaching, the need to get somewhere safe to hide was growing every minute. John could easily have woken up already. When the horse had shied, for one horrible moment, she'd thought it had been John sitting up there, before she remembered that John would be too drunk to ride.

"Hurry up and decide, won't you?" the man interrupted, a little gruffly. "I've been hankering to get to the ranch for days!"

Chloe looked up at him, her eyes meeting his. Getting to her feet, she picked up her valise and tried to smile. "Thank you," she murmured. "I guess I'll come to the ranch."

He eyed her for a moment longer, before jumping down from his horse and taking her bag from her. She looked fit to drop and the last thing he wanted was an unconscious woman on his hands. "Up you go," he grinned, dropping her bag and holding out his coupled hands for her foot. "Before you faint."

Pulling herself up on the horse, Chloe felt a rush of relief flood her, making her sag slightly.

"We won't be long," he continued, smiling up at her with only a faint trace of worry. "I'm Michael, by the way."

"Chloe," she replied, her voice barely loud enough for him to hear.

"Well, Chloe," he smiled briskly, leading the horse on. "Let's get on to the ranch."

Chapter Three: "Meet the Family"

Michael had barely been able to take his eyes off Chloe as they made their way to the ranch. She was sitting as tall as she could, despite her apparent exhaustion. Her dark curls bounced as she rode, highlighting just how pale she was. Occasionally, he would see her glancing all around, as though fearful of what she might see. Was she worried about someone coming after her? And if so, who? He didn't want to ask her, not on such a short acquaintance. There would be time for all that later.

Now, they both stood at the front door of the ranch, waiting for someone to let them in. Chloe was trembling slightly, although she hoped he couldn't see it. She was half expecting John to appear at the door, even though she knew they were far away from his place.

"Michael!"

A friendly looking man appeared at the door, immediately pulling Michael into a bear hug. Chloe hung back as the two men laughed and hugged, both talking at once.

"It's great to see you," Michael chuckled,

truly happy to see his older brother again. "You haven't changed a bit!"

"This place agrees with me," Christopher replied with a grin. "As does my wife! Speaking of, come in and I'll introduce you." His eyes suddenly caught sight of Chloe, who was trying to hide in the shadow of the door. "Oh, I'm terribly sorry," he continued, immediately. "I didn't know Michael was bringing a bride of his own!" He threw a questioning look at his brother as Chloe felt her cheeks grow hot.

Michael tried to laugh, although the sound stuck in his throat. "Not my bride, Michael. I found her on the way here, she's looking for some help."

"I'm sorry to be a bother," Chloe said, wishing she could make her voice louder than the whisper it currently was. "But I really had nowhere else to go."

Christopher's eyes grew sympathetic. "Of course. Come in, Chloe. You're very welcome, and I'm sure my wife, Eliza, will be more than happy to help you."

"Thank you."

Chloe threw a quick look at Michael, whose lips had curved into a smile, as he stood back to let her enter in front of him. He was quite the gentleman, she thought to herself, as she walked into the house. Her heart was beating so fast and so loudly, she thought she might collapse right there and then.

Michael caught sight of Chloe swaying just a little as she walked in, and gently rested his hand on her lower back, supporting her as they made their way into the kitchen. Looping his arm around her waist, he quickly guided her to a chair, before turning to meet his brother's new wife.

"Eliza," he smiled, as Christopher quickly made the introductions. "I'm really pleased to meet you."

She smiled back, before giving him a quick hug. "We're family now," she laughed, catching his surprised expression. "And I'm mighty pleased to meet you. This is Alice, she lives here with us."

"Nice to meet you," Michael replied, with a quick smile to the older lady sitting in the corner, busy with her knitting. "I'm sure glad to have made it!"

"We are too," Eliza smiled, glancing at Christopher. "We've got plenty going on at this ranch that we'll need help with — especially now that a certain someone will be making their appearance in a few months!"

Christopher kissed his wife's cheek, throwing an arm around her waist and tugging her closer. "Seems like we'll be expecting a baby in a few months time."

Michael's mouth dropped open in surprise.

"Congratulations!"

"You seem surprised!" Christopher laughed.

"I just got used to the idea of you being married," Michael retorted, throwing himself into a chair by the kitchen table. "And now you're telling me you're having a baby! I'm delighted, though."

"You'll be an uncle," Eliza replied, smiling. "I just want you to know how grateful we are that you're here."

"I sure hope you're planning to stay," Christopher asked, a little cautiously. "There's an old cabin on the other side of the corral. It's yours if you want it."

Michael couldn't help his astonishment. "You're offering me a place to live?"

"Well, if you're happy enough to repair it, then yes," Eliza replied, with a quiet smile. "We're glad to have you here, Michael. Family is important."

"Then I can't thank you enough," Michael said, softly. After some time wandering, he finally felt as though he was getting the chance to put down some roots – and to be offered a home of his own on his sister in law's ranch was more than he'd ever hoped for. "I'll be making myself useful though, don't you worry."

Just then, Eliza spotted Chloe and realised just how rude she'd been. "Oh, I'm dreadfully sorry! Here I am prattling away and I've not even introduced myself!"

Heat rippled into Chloe's cheeks as four pairs of eyes turned to her. "I'm so sorry for imposing on your hospitality."

"Don't mention that at all," Eliza declared, handing her a cup of tea. "Any friend of Michael's is welcome here."

"I'm not a friend, I'm afraid," Chloe replied, daring a glance at her rescuer. "Michael just found me out in the plains."

"Oh?"

She swallowed hard, knowing she was going to have to explain the truth. "I suppose I should start from the beginning."

Eliza sat down in a chair, a kind smile on her face. "Take your time, Chloe. Whenever you're ready."

Chapter Four: "Happy to Help"

Chloe took a deep breath, hoping that they weren't going to throw her out once they'd heard her story.

"I came to marry John, as a mail order bride."

"John Black, the farmer?" Christopher interrupted, frowning.

Chloe nodded, a little shamefaced. "Yes, that's him."

"What's the matter with him?" Eliza asked her husband, spotting the look of disgust on his face.

Christopher shook his head. "Not a good man, by all accounts. Don't care much for his animals and can barely get anyone to work for him. Got a bit of a bad reputation, he does."

"Oh dear," Alice piped up, from the corner. "Did you know anything about this before you came here, my dear?"

"No, I didn't," Chloe whispered, shame burning her cheeks. "I believed everything he told me about himself. He made himself out to be a hard working, honest man. He told me wonderful stories about life out here, and painted a glorious picture of the life we'd be living together."

"What a despicable man," Eliza declared, decisively. "You did not marry him then, I hope?"

Chloe shook her head. "I didn't, but I signed a contract before I arrived, promising that I would do so." A silence fell across the room as they realised what she meant. If there was a contract, then she was practically bound to the man, unless she could find a sympathetic judge who would release her from it. "Is the judge here kind?"

"There is no judge," Christopher replied. "There's one that comes around from time to time, but no-one permanent."

Michael cleared his throat. "So, if you ain't married, then why were you running away?"

Chloe pressed her lips together before answering, stemming the trembling in her hands. "I had nowhere else to go, so he took me to his farmhouse, promising we'd be married the next day. Once I realised that he wasn't who he'd said and that he had no intention of taking me to the pastor, I began to look for a way to escape."

"He didn't let you out of the house?" Eliza gasped, her hand going to her mouth.

Shaking her head, Chloe saw the spark of anger in Michael's eyes and felt herself grow a little calmer. He didn't seem to view her as in any kind of wrongdoing, in running away from her fiancé. "The moment I saw him drinking, I knew that was my only chance. I didn't know where to go but I knew I had to leave."

"Couldn't you have taken your contract with you?" Christopher asked, thoughtfully. "Without the contract, he's got no reason to bother you."

"He's hidden it somewhere," she explained, shaking her head. "I couldn't dare look for it in case he woke up. Besides," she continued, stammering a little. "I – I was sure he'd begin to....press his attentions on me even more, if I stayed." She shuddered, her eyes dropping to the floor.

"You're safe here," Eliza said, kindly. "Don't you get yourself all het up now, Chloe. He won't find you here, and, even if he comes knocking, Michael and Christopher will send him packing."

"Thank you," Chloe whispered, gratefully. "I only wish I could get that contract. Then I would be truly free."

Michael said nothing but began to grow hot with anger over how the lady had been treated. She was clearly exhausted and terrified, and he felt a slight frisson of guilt shake him as he realised just how gruff he'd been with her. She was a strong woman, enduring what she had, and still managing to escape. Right now, he wanted to go up to John Black's farm and shake him until his teeth rattled. Then he'd throw him a punch or two, demand the contract and burn it in front of his face.

"And then get sent to jail," he muttered to himself, closing his eyes briefly.

As Eliza and Alice began to reassure Chloe,

Christopher leant over to his brother. "Now don't you go getting yourself caught up doing something stupid, little brother."

"What are you talking about?" Michael grunted, in frustration."

"I see that look on your face, no matter how quickly you try to hide it," Christopher grinned. "That woman's got a hold of you already. Just don't go stomping up to John's place, like I know you probably want to."

Michael opened his mouth to tell his brother just how wrong he was, only for Christopher to slap him on the back, push himself away from the wall and walk over to his wife.

"Chloe, you are welcome to stay with us for as long as it takes to get things sorted," Christopher declared, with a smile. "Alice, you don't mind sharing your room, do you?"

"Not at all," Alice declared, with a smile. "We'll be cosy but comfortable, Chloe, don't you worry."

Michael realised, with a jolt, that he was now going to be under the same roof as this Chloe, surprised at how delighted he was by the news. Maybe he'd get to know Chloe a little more, and find out what it was that had drawn her to this place. Something in him wanted to help her, to make her smile instead of frown.

Chapter Five "Come With Me"

Chloe smiled to herself as she stirred the stew. She'd been here for five days now and was slowly beginning to relax. There hadn't been any sightings of John, and she was throwing herself into helping out at the ranch where she could. For the time being, they'd thought it best that she stay inside, but Chloe had only been too glad to agree. Helping out with the chores had been second nature, and since Chloe was a keen cook, she'd been glad to help Alice and Eliza out. Eliza, unfortunately, was suffering badly with morning sickness, and both Chloe and Alice had insisted that she rest. It wasn't like Eliza to stay in bed, but at their cajoling – and at Christopher's insistence – she'd eventually done as they'd asked.

"That smells good."

Chloe looked around, smiling at Michael as he walked in, taking his hat from his head. He smiled at her and immediately, a warm glow spread from her core to the very tips of her fingers. She couldn't help her reaction to him. He'd always spend a few minutes speaking to her during the day, just finding out how her day was going. Chloe felt a chuckle rise in her throat as she thought of how badly she'd reacted to him the first time they'd met, in the middle of the desert plains. He'd been gruff and frustrated, and she'd not been sure whether to trust him or not. Now, he was the exact opposite, friendly and charming with a smile that always seemed to spark something inside her.

Stirring the stew, Chloe gave him a quick smile. "I hope you're hungry."

"Sure am," he grinned, sitting down in one of the chairs by the table. "Been out working with the horses today. Adam and Susanna were showing me their way to gentle a feisty mare."

Chloe smiled. She'd been introduced to Susanna yesterday, who was betrothed to Adam, one of the hardest working ranch hands. They'd both been very friendly to her and Chloe had warmed to them both at once. It seemed that Susanna was quite an unusual woman, given her deep affinity for animals and her skill with them. "I'd love to see them soon."

"Susanna and Adam? Or the horses?"

She laughed. "Yes, the horses. I haven't been outside since you found me and it's growing a little tiresome."

He grinned. "I'll take you now if you like?"

A worried look crossed her face. "Now? Oh, I'm not sure if it'll be safe. John might – "

"We'll keep to the barn," he promised. "So even if John does turn up, he won't see you."

"I have the stew," Chloe continued, a little helplessly. The thought of going outside made her stomach clench with nerves, as though John might spot her the moment she put a foot outdoors, but at the same time, she was keen to have a little more freedom.

"I can do that," Alice piped up, walking in just as Chloe finished speaking. "Going outside, are you?"

"Yes," Chloe replied, realising she had no other option but to agree. "Just to the barn though."

Alice nodded fervently. "Very wise," she murmured, taking the wooden spoon from Chloe's hand. "That husband of yours has been looking for you in town, or so I've heard."

Chloe stopped still. "He has?"

Alice glanced at her, her face tightening as she realised Chloe hadn't been told. "Ah. I see I shouldn't have told you. Christopher probably didn't want to worry you."

"What did he hear?" Chloe asked, her heart thumping in her chest.

Alice shrugged. "You'd better go ask him. It'll be better coming from him."

"Come on," Michael murmured, slipping a strong arm around her shoulders as Chloe's face lightened just a shade. "Christopher's in the barn. We'll go talk to him together."

The moment Chloe stepped outside, she couldn't help but smile. The fresh air filled her lungs and she tipped her face to the sun for a moment. "Oh, this is wonderful!"

Michael's hand moved to her waist, although he stepped to the side just a little, to get a better look at her. "You've missed this."

"I always enjoyed being outdoors," Chloe murmured, suddenly very aware of his arm around her waist. "I've missed the sun and the wind on my face."

He smiled, before dropping his hand completely. She missed the contact at once, aware that the heat in her cheeks was from more than just the sunshine. "Want to go see the horses?"

"Oh yes," she replied, smiling. "But I'd like to speak to Christopher first, if I can."

"He'll still be in the corral, working with the horses," Michael replied, holding out his hand to her as though it were second nature. "Lets go find him."

Chloe paused for just a moment, before slipping her hand in his. It was just friendliness, she told herself as she walked down the steps and across to the corral. There wasn't anything more to it.

Besides, until she got that contract back from John, she couldn't contemplate a future with anyone. Marriage would be out of the question if she'd promised herself to another man. The only way she could start again would be to leave this place and go far, far away to where no-one knew her. Perhaps there she could find a husband of her own.

The thought of leaving sent a swift stab of pain through her heart, as Michael glanced down at her with a smile. He was so different from John and already, Chloe had to admit, her heart beat a little faster when he smiled at her.

Michael caught sight of Christopher but didn't quicken his pace. He quite liked the feel of Chloe's hand in his and hadn't missed the way her big brown eyes had flickered with an unspoken desire when she'd taken it. It was the same spark he felt in his own heart.

Chapter Six:"Hiding"

Michael leant on the wooden fence of the corral and smiled. Chloe was already busy getting to know the horses, and Susanna had been more than happy to help her with the introductions. Her tinkling laugh carried over to his ears and his smile widened.

"Don't tell me you're getting sweet on her," said a voice in his ear.

Michael jumped, turning to glare at his brother. "No."

"There's no shame in falling in love, Michael," Christopher replied, suddenly serious. "She seems like a sweet lady."

"She is," Michael retorted before he could stop himself. "But that don't mean nothing," he finished, lamely.

Christopher chuckled, slapping him on the back. "You're sunk," he grinned. "Just as well you're fixing up that old place. You'll need a home of your own when you're married."

Michael wanted to tell him to shut up and that he wasn't even thinking of marrying anyone, let along Chloe, but right then, Chloe's eyes met his and suddenly he couldn't even think straight. Heat rushed through him as she sent a soft smile his way, before turning back to the horses. The idea of marrying her suddenly didn't seem like such a bad idea.

Michael had always thought about settling down and marrying one day, he just hadn't thought it would be anytime soon. But Christopher was right, now he had a home of his own, although it needed a lot of work, and he could just picture Chloe by his side with maybe a handful of kids around them. It was an almost idyllic picture, but not one he could push away all that quickly.

The only thing that stood in his way was that contract that tied Chloe to John. If he had it, he could show it to any authority and Chloe wouldn't have any other choice but to return to him. It was almost like a marriage, except without the vows. Plenty mail order brides did it these days, just so that their prospective husbands wouldn't be able to turn them away immediately. He'd heard that, on occasions, the man and woman had decided to rip up the contract together, before going their separate ways, but he wondered just how many women were like Chloe – trapped, with no way out.

A sudden sound of hooves made him frown, turning his head to look.

"It's John," Christopher growled, stepping closer to Michael. "I'd recognise that horse of his anywhere." The mount was certainly striking, with its red coat, about the colour of a new penny. There weren't many horses around these parts with that colouring, Michael guessed.

"I need to get Chloe out of here," he mumbled, pulling his hat firmly down on his head.

"Get her into the barn," Christopher said, his eyes on John. "No doubt he'll want to come looking, so once he's inside the house, maybe take her to your place. I'll come find you once he's gone."

Michael wanted to comment that his place was practically falling down around his ears, but chose not to, climbing the corral fence instead.

"It's John," he said quietly, catching Chloe's gasp of fright. "Come with me, Chloe. Take one of the horses with you for cover."

Chloe's lip trembled, but she did exactly what Michael said, leading one of the horses back towards the barn, putting the animal between herself and the house. John wouldn't catch sight of her, not if she was careful.

Once inside the barn, Chloe hid in one of the dark corners, peeping through a slight gap in the wall. "It *is* John," she breathed, trying not to feel afraid. "I knew I should have stayed in the house!"

Michael snorted, coming to stand next to her. "No, you shouldn't have. That man can't run your life for you."

"If he has the contract, he can," Chloe said, with a slight sob. "I don't know what I'm going to do, Michael!"

He wrapped an arm around her waist and

pulled her close. "Don't worry, Chloe. We'll get that contract back, just you wait and see." A plan was slowly forming in his mind, but he couldn't put word to it just yet.

"Really?" she whispered, her moisture-filled eyes looking up at him.

Michael felt something begin to swirl inside him as he looked back down at her. "Really, Chloe," he murmured, his eyes drifting from her brown orbs to her lips. "I promise you won't be tied to him forever."

Chloe didn't know what was happening to her. She couldn't look away from Michael, even if she'd wanted to. His green eyes were mesmerising, his words so full of promise that she desperately wanted to believe him. Instead of feeling afraid about John, all she could think of was just how close Michael was to her, and how intimate an embrace they were in.

"We'd, uh, best keep watching," he murmured, eventually, breaking the spell. "John might want to search the barn, so the minute he goes in the house, we have to run to my place."

"Your place?" Chloe asked, with a frown, "Oh, you mean the old house on the ranch you've been fixing up?"

"Right," he replied, dropping his hand from her waist. "It's only been a couple of weeks so there's not much done, but it's safe and secure. Christopher won't let him come looking."

Chloe gave him a quick smile, thinking just

how safe and secure she felt when he was around. There was something about him that gave her reassurance, that seemed to calm her very soul. "How far away is it?"

"Far enough that John won't come looking," he promised, hoping that she'd be okay with walking to the other side of the ranch. He'd been working there earlier in the day and had water there so they wouldn't be thirsty. The thought of being alone with her in his house sent a ricochet of excitement into his heart, curling down into his belly, but Michael only cleared his throat, gave her a quick smile and carried on watching John.

Chapter Seven: "Unexpected Kisses"

Chloe took in great heaving gasps of air, feeling her lungs burning. The moment John had entered the house, they'd taken off across the corral, running towards the old house at the other end of the ranch. Chloe couldn't remember the last time she'd run that fast, and it had only been the fear that John would see her that had kept her going.

"Here," Michael said, handing her a jar of water. "Drink this, Chloe." He watched her take huge gulps of water, thinking that she looked quite exhausted. "You did really well, Chloe. We're safe here, for now."

"You don't think he saw us?"

Michael shook his head. "They'd have kept him away from the windows, just to be safe. Christopher will come and get us when he's gone."

Chloe sat down on a rickety looking old chair. "How long will that be?"

He shrugged. "Not too long, hopefully. I've got some food here if you're hungry."

Thanking him, Chloe shook her head. She didn't think she could face food at the moment. The knowledge that John was on the Martin Ranch was making her stomach churn, while the rest of her body was on fire from being so close to Michael. There had been a spark between them that had almost had her kissing him desperately, but she'd stopped herself in time. She wasn't even sure how he felt about her, although from the way she caught him looking at her from time to time, Chloe wondered if he was as attracted to her as she was to him.

Michael sat down opposite her, on the only other chair in the place, and propped his feet up on the old table. "Guess we can relax here for a while."

Chloe laughed, shaking her head at him. "I don't know if relaxed is the right word!" Looking around the place, she saw the tools and things lying about. "How are you getting on with the house?"

He shrugged. "It's going to take a long time, but I'm starting to get there. The first thing to do is to fill up all the holes and replace the old wood with new. Make it windproof and watertight." This place was dry and dusty, but when it rained, it rained hard.

"It looks like it has a lot of potential," Chloe said, softly.

"That it does," Michael agreed. For a moment, he could see him sitting here with Chloe on the opposite side of the table, his ring on her finger. They'd have plaid curtains on the windows, and she'd be cooking a sweet smelling stew for dinner, just like the one she'd been making back at the ranch house.

Chloe smiled at him, aware of how toes curled when he smiled back. "Have you always wanted to work on the ranch?" Realising that she didn't know all that much about his past, Chloe found herself wondering about his past.

"Christopher and I were both ranch workers for years," he explained. "That was before I began to think that maybe life in the big ol' city was a better place to be." He grimaced. "Didn't take long to realise I'd made a mistake."

"So you came out here."

He nodded. "My brother was always good at looking out for me. I reckon I'll be here for the rest of my days."

Chloe tipped her head, studying him. "Are you happy about that?"

"Definitely," he grinned. "It's about time I settled down. Maybe take a wife, that sort of thing."

Her breath caught as his green eyes flicked to hers.

"How would you feel about living out here, Chloe?" he asked, quietly.

Chloe took a breath, trying to stop the sudden shaking in her hands. Michael was asking her one of the biggest questions she'd ever hand to answer. "I reckon I could live out here too," she whispered, as he pushed his chair back and got to his feet.

Walking around to her, Michael threw

caution to the wind and pulled her into his arms. "Chloe, I can't get you out of my mind," he whispered before he bent his head.

Completely surprised about everything that had just happened, Chloe could barely breathe, let alone think. The suddenness of the way he'd pulled her from her seat and began kissing her had almost made her numb with shock – but a swift wave of heat soon flooded her. His lips were soft but demanding, urging her to respond. Chloe had never felt anything like this before, sagging against him as delight and pleasure began to wash over her. Tentatively, she wrapped her arms around his neck and let her fingers twine into his hair, inciting a slight groan from Michael.

"Did I hurt you?" she gasped, pulling back, but Michael only shook his head before putting his lips back on hers again. He couldn't get enough of her.

Michael wasn't sure what had come over him but the way Chloe had looked at him from across the table had demanded a response. The surge of desire had practically forced him from his seat until now, he was kissing her smooth lips and slipping his hands around her waist. She was soft and warm, almost hesitant in the way she was responding. Michael was sure she'd never kissed anyone before, but there was a passion in her response that echoed in his own heart. He wanted Chloe. Wanted this. Wanted a happy and fulfilling life here on the ranch, with Chloe by his side. It was almost crazy how much he felt for her, after only a few weeks of acquaintance, but it couldn't be denied. It wasn't just a sensual desire, but a deep longing for her that was etching its way inside his heart. He cared about her and wanted nothing more but to take her away from John. *She shouldn't be with him, she should be with me,* he thought to himself as he kissed her again, almost overcome with everything he felt.

"We need to stop," he said, eventually, stepping away from her embrace. His breathing was ragged, while her breath came in short gasps. "We need to talk, Chloe."

She nodded, her hands trembling as she pulled back out her chair and sat down. Her legs felt like water and her whole body was shaking with emotion. No-one had ever kissed her like that. There had been so much passion in it, so much feeling that it almost scared her. Michael was right. They needed to talk.

Chapter Eight: "A Proposal"

Michael ran a hand through his hair over and over again, trying to get his heart to calm its frantic pace. Everything was going so fast, but Michael realised he'd never felt surer of anything in his life. Having Chloe here with him, in the home that was going to be his, was possibly the best idea he'd ever had. She just seemed to 'fit'. "Chloe," he began, sitting down opposite her. "You are amazing." He watched as her eyes flickered with surprise, followed by a light blush to her cheeks.

"Thank you." If she was honest, Chloe would admit that he made her feel like that way. "John spent most of the time telling me how useless I was and, after a while, it was hard not to believe him."

"Don't even think about what that man said about you," he replied, almost snarling at the thought. "You're one amazing woman, Chloe. That's why I want you to stay here, with me."

She swallowed, studying his face. "Are you....asking me to marry you?"

He let out a long breath, before smiling at

her gently. "Yeah, I guess I am. I know it's not the best proposal you've ever had, and I know we've only known each other for a few weeks but I like you, Chloe."

The smile on her face faded just a little. "I like you too, Michael," she said, slowly. "But you're right, this is going awfully fast." It wasn't as though Chloe had set her heart on marrying for love, but she didn't want to be in a marriage where they both only *liked* each other. There had to be something more, or at least the potential of it. That had been the reason she'd come to marry John. They'd grown close over their many letters, although everything he'd told her had then been shown to be untrue, the very moment she arrived. Biting her lip, Chloe looked up at Michael again, who was waiting for her answer. "I think I will marry you, Michael," she said slowly. "But not straight away."

He lifted one eyebrow. "What do you mean?"

She pressed her lips together for a moment, hoping this wasn't going to make him withdraw his proposal. "I want us to get to know each other better. I mean, I don't know anything much about you, things a wife should know."

"Such as...?"

She lifted her shoulders, seeing his frustrated frown. "Things like, what your favourite meal is, or how many children you want. From the big things to the small things, I want to know you better."

Michael grimaced, but eventually conceded. She was right, he realised. They didn't know each other well at all, and it would be good her better. "How long?"

"A few months?" she asked, softly.

He let out a sigh. "Alright, three months it is. I suppose it gives me time to get this place fixed up!"

Relieved, Chloe let out a quiet laugh. "Exactly, although I'll be happy to help you where I can."

"Really?"

She nodded, a smile on her face. "It is going to be my home too, after all."

"I suppose it is," he mused, his heart almost dancing with happiness.

Chloe smiled at him for a moment, before her face suddenly darkened. "Although this doesn't solve the problem of John and my contract."

Michael's shoulders slumped. Talking about their future together had made him conveniently forget about the very reason they were hiding in his old ramshackle cabin in the first place. "Right," he mumbled, rubbing a hand over his eyes. "I'd forgotten about that." Thinking quickly, he glanced up at his now wife-to-be and saw the worry in her eyes.

"John could cause a whole heap of trouble with that contract, even if we do marry," Chloe replied, quietly. "I just can't think how to get it back."

"We don't need to get it back," he said, thoughtfully. "We just need to destroy it." Reaching across the table, he held out his hand and waited for her to take it. "I'll find it for you, Chloe. You need to be free from this."

She smiled at him, as his fingers caressed the back of her hand. "I don't want you to put yourself in any danger, Michael. John's not a man to be trifled with."

"Don't you worry," he promised. "I'll talk to Christopher and Eliza and we'll come up with something. They care about you too, you know."

Chloe nodded, knowing it was true. A sudden knock at the door had her squeal with fright, only for Michael to reassure her that it was probably only Christopher.

"Sorry," Christopher mumbled, looking a little embarrassed. "Didn't mean to frighten you there, Anna."

Her hand on her heart, Anna tried to tell him that it was okay, but could only take great whooshing gasps in an attempt to calm herself down.

"Has he gone?" Michael asked, quietly. He didn't want to panic Anna any more than she already was.

Christopher nodded, his face grave. "It ain't good, Michael. Says he's coming back with the sheriff and his men."

"Why?" Anna gasped, hearing him speak.

"Why would he do that? Does he know I'm here?"

Christopher took a deep breath. "We wouldn't let him come up here to check out this place, even though he wanted to."

"So now he's suspicious," Michael finished, shaking his head.

"Precisely."

"Then what are we going to do?" Anna whispered, her heart beginning to pound frantically.

Christopher and Michael both turned to her, wearing identical smiles of reassurance. "Don't worry," Michael replied, walking over to her and taking her ice-cold hand in his. "We'll come up with something. I told you we would. Christopher will help."

"Of course I will," Christopher agreed at once. "Come on, lets get you back to the ranch house. Eliza will be going frantic waiting to see you're alright!"

Chapter Nine: "We Need a Plan"

Eliza threw her arms around Chloe the moment she walked in. "Are you okay, Chloe?"

"I'm fine," Chloe replied, smiling. The walk back to the ranch house had been spent talking through ideas with both Christopher and Michael and now she felt quite reassured. There would be a way out of this for her, there *had* to be.

"We were quite worried," Alice interrupted, ladling stew into bowls. "The moment John said he wanted to search all the outbuilding..."

"Well, yes," Christopher continued, throwing Alice a warning glance. "But he's gone now and we have time to come up with a plan."

Eliza frowned. "A plan? What kind of plan?"

Chloe glanced at Michael, a slight blush hitting her cheeks. "Michael and I are....well, we've decided that – "

"I'm going to marry her," Michael interrupted, a wide grin on his face.

Silence filled the room as three pairs of eyes stared at Michael before moving to Chloe. Chloe felt herself grow hot all over they gazed at her. She couldn't tell whether they were pleased or just in shock.

"Well, somebody say something!" Michael exclaimed, after a moment. "It's sudden, I know, but we won't be marrying for a few months yet. We need to get to know one another a bit better first."

Eliza threw her arms around Chloe once more, breaking the silence. "How wonderful! I'm so happy for you, Chloe."

"Thank you," Chloe murmured, as she pulled back from Eliza's embrace – only to find herself in Alice's arms.

"This is wonderful news," Alice continued, hugging Chloe. "I knew the moment you two walked in the door something like this would happen."

"Really?" Chloe asked, leaning back to look in Alice's face. "You could tell?"

"Of course I could," Alice smiled, patting her grey hair. "You don't get hair this colour without having seen a few things, and if it's one thing I know it's when a man's in love."

Chloe felt her heart drop to her toes before racing back up to her chest. Michael hadn't mentioned the word love to her, and neither had she to him. She certainly had feelings for him, but she wasn't really sure whether or not they would grow to love. It was almost a relief to hear Alice's words.

Christopher slapped Michael on the shoulder. "I hope you know what you're getting yourself in for," he grinned.

"Seems to suit you," Michael quipped, his

eyes on Chloe.

"It does," Christopher replied, looking over at his wife who gave him a soft smile. "Chloe seems like a good woman, Michael. I hope you're going to do your best to make her happy."

"I will," Michael said, fervently. "The only problem now is the contract."

A few minutes later, the group were sitting around the table, with dinner in front of them and their heads full of thoughts. After the news of Michael and Chloe's engagement had sunk in, they'd then all realised that the obstacle standing in front of their impending happiness was John and his contract.

"Could you just ask him for it?" Alice asked, shrugging. "Maybe if he knows Chloe and Michael want to marry, then that will change his mind."

Chloe shook her head. "John doesn't care about me. As far as he's concerned, I belong to him. Nothing's going to change that."

Christopher sighed. "From what I saw of John today, I think I agree. He's determined to get Chloe back no matter what."

"So, you have to get rid of the contract then," Eliza said, practically.

"We can't just ride up and get it," Michael retorted, a little exasperated. "Or I'd have done that by now."

Eliza tilted her head. "But what if his house was empty? You could search his house then, knowing that he wasn't there."

Chloe sat up a little straighter, her mind working hard. "He's coming back here, isn't he? With the sheriff?"

"Yes, tomorrow I think," Christopher replied, slowly. "So his house would be entirely empty."

"And Chloe can't be here," Michael warned, aware that the sheriff and his men would do a thorough search.

"Then I'll go with you," Chloe said, quietly.

"What do you mean, go with me?"

Feeling everyone's eyes on her, Chloe tried to explain quickly. "John and the sheriff don't know that you're here, do they, Michael?"

"No, they don't." He studied Chloe as she spoke, watching the way her face became more and more animated. Clearly, she'd come up with a plan.

"Then when the sheriff arrives, we ride up to John's house and search for the contract," she explained. "I'm not sure where we'd hide or anything, since I don't know the area very well, but we'd know that John would be here."

"And that would give us time to look for and find the contract," Michael finished, a small smile breaking out. "You're amazing, Chloe." His face filled with admiration for her and Chloe felt her cheeks grow hot, as warmth spread through her.

"You'll have to hide out of sight," Christopher warned. "Maybe take two horses to the top of the hill and stay there. You should have a good vantage point. It might be dangerous, though. What if John comes back to the house early?"

"I trust Michael to keep me safe," Chloe murmured, softly, her eyes on her fiancé's.

"Then it's settled," Michael grinned, thumping the table with his fist for good measure. "First thing tomorrow, I'll get the horses ready and then all we'll have to do is wait."

"It sounds like you've got a plan," Alice murmured, from her corner of the table. "Just be careful, both of you."

Chapter Ten: "Let's Go!"

"Nervous?"

Chloe looked over at Michael and nodded. There was no point in pretending. She'd barely slept last night, tossing and turning and worrying about John and that blasted contract.

"Don't be," Michael smiled, trying to reassure her. "We'll find it."

"I hope so." This was her only chance of freedom. "What happens if he's got it in his pocket, or something?"

Michael shook his head. "Something that precious? No, he won't keep it on him. Too risky that way. He might lose it, when he's riding or something. He'll have it somewhere safe in the house."

Chloe took a breath, watching as John, the sheriff and some other men walked up to the ranch house. They were well out of sight, just waiting for the right time.

"Looks like they're heading for it," Michael murmured. "Did you manage to hide all your things?"

"Yes, I did. Put them in with Alice and Eliza's particulars. The men won't dare search there."

Michael chuckled. Eliza could be something of a spitfire when she wanted and there was no way any man was going to start going through a woman's things. "They've gone in," he said, pulling Chloe to her feet and catching her in his arms when she stumbled.

They looked at each other for a moment, the world going quiet. Michael's heart began to slam into his chest as he gazed into Chloe's eyes, forgetting about everything they were meant to be doing. When he kissed her gently, she responded quickly, pulling him closer by twining her arms around his neck.

"Chloe," he rumbled, after a moment. "You bewitch me." Giving her one final, swift kiss, he grinned at the blush on her cheeks before helping her into the saddle. "We'd best ride hard," he said, leaping onto his own horse. "Before they come out the ranch house and see us. Ready?"

Chloe nodded, digging her heels into the horse's sides and following Michael across the plain.

A short time later, and John's farmhouse came into view. The sight of it turned Chloe's stomach, and she could feel the blood draining from her face. She hated this place. It had been the place where her dreams had shattered, where she'd thought she'd never escape.

"You okay?" Michael asked, softly, seeing the pain in her expression.

"Not really," she replied, her voice shaking. "I'll be alright in a moment."

He nodded, taking them both around the back of the house and behind the barn. "Best tie them here," he said, jumping down. "They won't be seen easily."

Chloe jumped down herself, not waiting for his help, but he pulled her into his arms anyway.

"I know you're scared," he whispered, feeling her tremble. "But you don't need to be. I'm right here with you. You won't ever have to go back with him, I promise."

"What if we don't find the contract?"

"Then I'll take you away from here," he promised, leaning back to look into her face. "We'll marry somewhere else, somewhere knew." The look on her face made his heart ache. She looked so scared, so vulnerable. "I swear I'll protect you, Chloe."

"Thank you, Michael," Chloe whispered, letting his strength fill her. The fact that he was willing to start over, just to keep her away from John, spoke volumes. No-one had ever cared for her that way before.

"Come on," he murmured, stepping away and taking her hand. "Let's go."

The house was dark and dusty, making Chloe cough as they began to search.

Michael shook his head at the state of the place. "How can he live like this?" he asked, to no-one in particular. The house was littered with dirty plates and crockery, with clothes flung everywhere and even empty bottles lying on the floor. Some books were stacked haphazardly on the kitchen table and the curtains didn't look like they'd been opened for weeks. A thin layer of dust lay over most things and there was a musty scent in the air.

"I had to clean this place every day," Chloe mumbled, remembering how lazy John had been. "The man did nothing." She didn't know how John survived as a farmer, given how little he seemed to do. Michael, on the other hand, was the exact opposite. Out before the sun rose, working hard on getting his home fixed up and on helping Christopher and Eliza. She could never have been happy with John. He wasn't what she – or what any woman – needed.

"Any idea where to start looking?"

Chloe shook her head. "The bedroom's there, but I'd prefer if you searched it if you don't mind." The last thing she wanted to see was John's unmentionables lying around.

Michael nodded, understanding her reticence. "I'll be as quick as I can. Make sure you come and tell me if you hear any noises."

"Sure will." Chloe watched as Michael disappeared into the bedroom, before taking another long look around the house. Panic and fear were making her heart begin to thump loudly, but Chloe pushed those feelings away. She had to think calmly and carefully.

Chloe began a thorough search of the living area but didn't find anything. Flicking through the books on the table, she choked at the amount of dust that came off them, putting them back carefully. There was nothing under the rug or in the empty drinks bottles on the floor. His liquor cabinet – while well stocked – didn't have any hiding places and neither was there anything in the chest of drawers. Sighing heavily, Chloe glanced through a crack in the curtains, just to make sure no-one was coming. There wasn't a single sound, and Chloe took in a long breath, trying to calm her frantically beating heart.

Wandering into the kitchen, she began to look around. Dust covered almost everything and stagnant water was in a couple of pots. The sight turned her stomach. Goodness knows what John had been eating since she was gone, but whatever it was, he certainly hadn't cleaned up after himself.

"Where could it be?" she murmured to herself, thinking hard. John hated cooking, that was for sure, so why were some pots sitting to one side, looking as though they'd just been cleaned. In fact, they were the only things that were shining in the entire kitchen. Everything else was either dusty or dirty. "Michael?" she called, hearing him come running out. "Look."

Chapter Eleven: "This is Over!"

"What am I looking at?"

Chloe quickly explained, walking over to them. "It doesn't make sense for these to be so clean." The three pans were neatly stacked on top of each other, with the lid under each pot for balance. Grasping the small one, Chloe handed it to Michael, who looked inside but gave a shake of his head.

"This one?" she asked, handing him the second one as she looked inside the third.

"No," he said, softly. "Nothing. Sorry, Chloe."

"There's nothing in this one either," she sighed, her heart sinking. "I thought that was such a good idea."

Just as Michael handed her the second pot to put back, Chloe froze for a moment, her eyes catching sight of something.

"Lift that up again," she cried, excitedly.

"Lift what up?" Michael asked, a puzzled look on his face.

"The bottom of the pot!" Chloe exclaimed. As Michael turned it over, Chloe's hands flew to her mouth as she caught her breath. There it was.

The contract.

"Is this it?" Michael asked, delicately unsticking the piece of paper from the bottom of the pot, before unfolding it.

Chloe nodded, a sudden rush of tears in her eyes. "Yes, that's it," she whispered. "I'd recognise it anywhere."

Michael's eyes darted across the few written lines, as Chloe pointed out her signature. Relief flooded him, and he pulled Chloe in to his chest. "You found it," he whispered, pressing a kiss to her temple. "You're free, Chloe."

Chloe gazed up at him, her heart filled with gratitude. She knew she would never have dared to come back here without his help. He had offered her more than just her freedom, he had offered her a future. A bright one, filled with life and laughter. "I couldn't have done this without you, Michael," she whispered, as his thumb brushed tears from her cheek. "Thank you."

As they shared a brief kiss, a sudden sound made them both freeze. Chloe felt her blood turn to ice in her veins as she heard John shouting out loud to himself, clearly frustrated.

"It's John," she mouthed, turning horror filled eyes on Michael. "What are we going to do?"

Michael thought fast. They couldn't get out of the house to get to the horses, not without John seeing them. "We have to face him, Chloe."

"No," she whispered, her hands scrabbling for a hold on his arm. "Michael, I can't!"

He kissed her, hard. "Yes, you can. We have the contract now, so there's nothing he can do. He doesn't have a hold over you, Chloe."

Chloe could feel herself shaking all over. The last thing in the world she wanted to do was go and face John, but it seemed she didn't have an option. They couldn't hide in his house, and they couldn't go out to get the horses without being spotted. "I'm scared, Michael."

"I'm right here with you," he promised, taking her hand. "Come on. Let's face him together."

Trying to stand tall, Chloe walked with Michael out of the house, clenching her free hand into a fist. Her fingernails bit into the palm of her hand, but she needed the pain to stay focused. Lifting her chin, she took a shaky breath and stepped outside.

"You!" John had spotted them immediately. "I've been looking all over for you!" His face was red, his arm shooting out to grab her arm, but Michael was there in a moment.

"No, you don't," he said, quietly. "Keep your hands off her, John."

John's face grew dark with rage. "Who are you and what are you doing with my wife?" he half shouted.

"I'm not your wife," Chloe replied, trying not to panic. "And I never will be, John."

"Is that so?" he sneered. "Well, I think otherwise. I've got that contract, remember?"

Chloe lifted one eyebrow. "Is that so?" she asked, softly. She watched as his eyes narrowed, only to flair in understanding. She saw the way his lip curled and his hands slowly clenched. Moving a little closer to Michael, she felt him wrap his arm around her shoulders, squeezing gently to encourage her.

"You've taken it, haven't you?" John swore out loud, his voice throbbing with anger. "Give it back."

"I don't know what you're talking about," Chloe whispered, trying to stay strong. "But if you can't find that contract, then you have no hold over me."

John snorted, shaking his head. "I'll get it back, don't you worry about that. Even if I have to fight you for it." His eyes moved to Michael as he spoke. He clearly knew that one of them had it and he had placed his bets on it being Michael.

"There ain't going to be any kind of fighting necessary," came a sudden voice. "I thought I'd come up to check on you, John, to make sure you were okay. Does anyone want to explain to me exactly what's going on?"

It was the sheriff.

Chloe didn't know whether to be relieved or terrified. The man held the power around here. He could send her back to John, without question.

"Don't worry," Michael whispered, feeling her tense up. "The sheriff's a good man. We just need to explain what's happened. Don't hold back."

The sheriff gave Chloe an assessing glance. "You must be John's wife."

She gasped. "I'm not his wife!"

Frowning, the sheriff glanced back at John, who was looking a little shamefaced. "You're not?"

"No," Chloe explained, her chest beginning to heave with emotion. "I came as a mail order bride, but he never married me."

"I was always intending to – "

"He kept me here for days. I wasn't allowed outside, I –" Tears flooded her eyes and Chloe had to cover her mouth to keep from sobbing aloud.

"There, there," the sheriff murmured, softly. "Seems like you've had a bit of a rough time of it, Miss Chloe. Why don't we start from the beginning? I want you to tell me everything."

Chapter Twelve

Chloe looked up at the sheriff, seeing the kind look on his face. Trying to wind her emotions back in, she took a few deep breaths before beginning.

"John and I wrote to each other for a long time. He seemed kind and friendly and promised me a new life out here. So, when he sent me the contract agreeing to marry him, I didn't hesitate."

"And now you're trying to get out of it," John shouted. "You ungrateful little – "

"That's enough," the sheriff interrupted, turning to John. "You keep that mouth of yours shut until I speak to you. You've already lied to me once, telling me she was your wife, so I won't be listening to you until I'm good and ready. Understand?"

Michael managed to hide the grin that spread across his face as John dropped his head and muttered something he couldn't quite hear. This wasn't going to go well for the man, he could tell, but Michael didn't care. He just wanted Chloe away from John for good.

"Please, continue my dear," the sheriff continued, after glaring at John. "So you signed the contract. What happened when you arrived? Why aren't you married to John?"

Chloe felt her anger rise as she answered the sheriff's question. "He told me we'd marry the following day so, having no other choice, I came here with him. Unfortunately, he never did. Instead, he kept me inside, didn't allow me to go out and forced me to work here like a slave."

The sheriff's eyebrows rose as he threw a quick look at John who was standing to one side, a slow flush creeping up his neck. "Is that so?"

"The only reason I got away was because he ended up stone drunk one night and I took my chance. Michael found me in the plains and took me to the Martin Ranch." Looking at the sheriff with desperation in her eyes, Chloe stepped forward. "Please, sir, I don't want to marry John. He's not the man he said he was."

The sheriff cleared his throat, turning to look at John. "Is this true, John?"

John glared at Chloe for a moment, before replying to the sheriff. "It doesn't matter what she wants, she signed the contract. She's bound to me."

"No!" Chloe cried. "I won't marry you, John. I love Michael!"

Michael's heart almost stopped in her chest as he stared at her. Only just realising what she'd said, Chloe turned back to face him, her eyes brimming with tears. "I love you, Michael," she repeated, softly. "I want to make my life with you."

"Chloe," he murmured, stepping forward so he could pull her into his embrace. "I love you too." As her tears fell, he hugged her close, as John spat in the dirt. "Sheriff, I'm going to be honest with you, we came here to get the contract. I don't think it's right that Chloe is bound to a man like John. The way he treated her says he's not a good man and he won't be a good husband."

As John spluttered, the sheriff held up a hand to silence him before turning back to Michael. "You have the contract?"

Michael nodded, pulling it from his pocket and handing it to the sheriff. Keeping one arm around Chloe's waist, he looked down at her with an encouraging smile before turning his gaze back to the sheriff. His heart thumped madly as the sheriff looked over it carefully.

Chloe felt as though she were standing on a knife edge. Right now, the sheriff could decide what her future life was going to be like and she was just waiting for judgement to fall. No matter what happened, Chloe knew that she would always love Michael and that, somehow, he'd take her away from John. Her heart beat with love for him. He was everything John was not, and more. He cared for her, wanted a future with her and Chloe knew she would be safe with him. "Please," she whispered. "I want to marry Michael."

The sheriff harrumphed for a moment, before holding the contract up. Very delicately, he tore the paper into two pieces, before folding it and tearing it again. Tossing the pieces to the wind, he turned back to John who was now shouting in frustration and anger.

"You deceived this woman, John," the sheriff determined. "How dare you keep her here, like a prisoner? I ought to fling you in the cells because of it! But instead, you're going to keep yourself here, live quietly and work hard. If I hear even a single thing about you bothering these two, or anyone else at the Martin Ranch, I'll have your hide. You hear me?"

John clenched his jaw, his hands balled into fists. For a moment it looked like he was going to rush at Michael and Chloe, but a warning look from the sheriff had him stopped in his tracks. "Fine," he bit out, his face dark and angry.

"Good," the sheriff replied. "Now get in your house while I talk to these two."

Chloe tried not to shrink back as John walked past her, feeling Michael's hand tighten on her waist. The moment she heard the door shut, she let out a huge breath of relief, turning grateful eyes on the sheriff.

"I can't thank you enough," she breathed, blinking hard against sudden tears.

"Let me know if he bothers you again," the sheriff replied, walking over and shaking Michael's outstretched hand. "And I sure hope I'm going to get an invitation to your wedding!"

Chloe laughed, blushing as Michael pressed a kiss to her cheek. "Of course you will."

"Thank you, sheriff," Michael replied, grinning broadly. "I can't tell you just how happy you've made me."

"Glad to hear it," the man said, with a smile of his own. "Now, you'd best get back to that ranch, I'm sure your brother will be waiting to hear all about what you've been up to."

Thanking him again, Chloe and Michael walked back over to their horses, hardly able to believe what had happened. Chloe felt a great sense of freedom, as though she was able to breathe properly for the first time.

"Are you happy?" Michael asked, softly.

"Happy?" Chloe replied, as his arms slipped around her waist. "Of course I'm happy. I'm so lucky to have met you, Michael. You've made me happier than I've ever been in my life before."

"That's exactly the way I feel about you," Michael replied, honestly. "I can't wait to spend the rest of my life with you by my side."

Chloe lifted her arms around his neck, their hearts beating as one. "I love you, Michael," she whispered, softly.

"And I love you," he replied before he kissed her with all the passion he felt.

www.ingramcontent.com/pod-product-compliance
Lightning Source LLC
LaVergne TN
LVHW041634070526
838199LV00052B/3354